Meet Maui

By Andrea Posner-Sanchez
Illustrated by the Disney Storybook Art Team

A special thanks to the wonderful people of the Pacific Islands for inspiring us on this journey as we bring the world of Moana to life.

A Random House PICTUREBACK® Book

Random House 🏠 New York

Copyright © 2017 Disney Enterprises, Inc. All rights reserved. Published in the United States by Random House Children's Books, a division of Penguin Random House LLC, 1745 Broadway, New York, NY 10019, and in Canada by Penguin Random House Canada Limited, Toronto, in conjunction with Disney Enterprises, Inc. Pictureback, Random House, and the Random House colophon are registered trademarks of Penguin Random House LLC.

randomhousekids.com

ISBN 978-0-7364-3738-7

Printed in the United States of America

10 9 8 7 6 5 4 3 2 1

This is Maui.

He is a shape-shifting demigod with a magical fishhook.

Maui has many tattoos. They represent all his incredible feats.

For example, he once lassoed the sun to stretch out the daylight

hours and stole fire from the gods to give to humans.

But many, many years ago, Maui did something he shouldn't have.

He stole the heart of Te Fiti, the mother island.

And then he lost the heart and his fishhook. Since then, a darkness has been spreading over the world.

Moana is from the island of Motunui. She learns the story about Maui and the heart of Te Fiti when she is a little girl.

The ocean thinks Moana is special. It gives Moana the heart of Te Fiti
so she can make things better.

When she is a teenager, Moana finds Maui.
"I am Moana of Motunui," she tells him.
"You will journey to Te Fiti and
restore the heart!"

Maui doesn't want to help. He takes Moana's boat and sails away.
Before long, the ocean swoops Moana up and places her on the boat!

"If you put the heart back and save the world, you'd be everybody's hero," Moana tells Maui.
He likes the sound of that! But first, he needs to find his fishhook.

Maui uses his **expert wayfinding skills** to sail
their boat away from a crowd of tiny coconut-armored bandits . . .

. . . **all the way to Lalotai,** the realm of monsters. Maui's fishhook is stuck on the shell of a fifty-foot crab monster that collects shiny objects!

Working together, Maui and Moana get the fishhook without being eaten or crushed.

At first, Maui has trouble using his magical fishhook because he has lost his confidence.
He shape-shifts into a bug and a pig without meaning to.

After a heart-to-heart talk with Moana,
Maui keeps practicing.
Soon all his skills are back.

Maui shape-shifts into a hawk and bravely flies toward Te Kā, an enormous monster of lava and ash. He has to get past Te Kā to reach Te Fiti and restore her heart.

"Go save the world!" Moana cheers.

But Maui is knocked right out of the sky.

The two friends don't give up. Maui uses his fishhook to block Te Kā's fiery fist as Moana sails past to reach Te Fiti. But Te Fiti is gone, and Moana can't find a place to put the heart. She realizes she needs to give the heart to Te Kā.

The islands are saved! **Maui and Moana are heroes!** They will be friends forever!

Maui watches proudly as
Moana calms Te Kā and places
the heart in the glowing spiral.
It works. **Te Kā transforms
back into Te Fiti!**